Clothes That Help

Written by Ann-Marie Parker

Clothes can help people.
Some clothes keep
people safe when
they work or play.
Sometimes people
wear a helmet
to keep them safe, too.

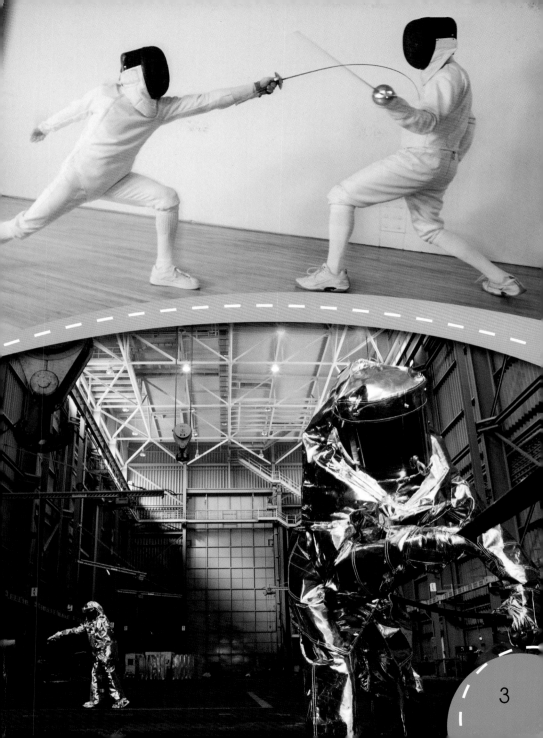

Astronauts wear
a space suit
when they are in space.
It can get very hot
or very cold in space.
The space suit helps
keep the astronaut
cool or warm.

helmet

space suit

The helmet helps
the astronaut breathe.

astronaut

A diver wears a wetsuit
under the water.
The suit keeps
the diver warm.
Divers wear masks to help
them see under the water.
Sometimes the mask can
help them breathe, too.

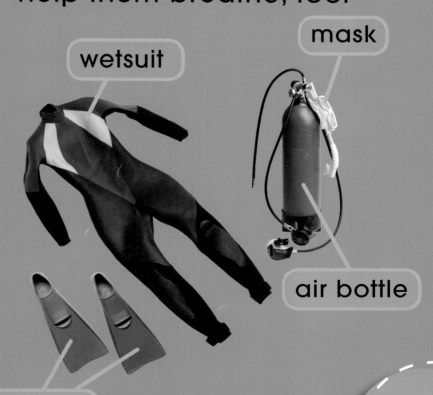

mask

wetsuit

air bottle

flippers

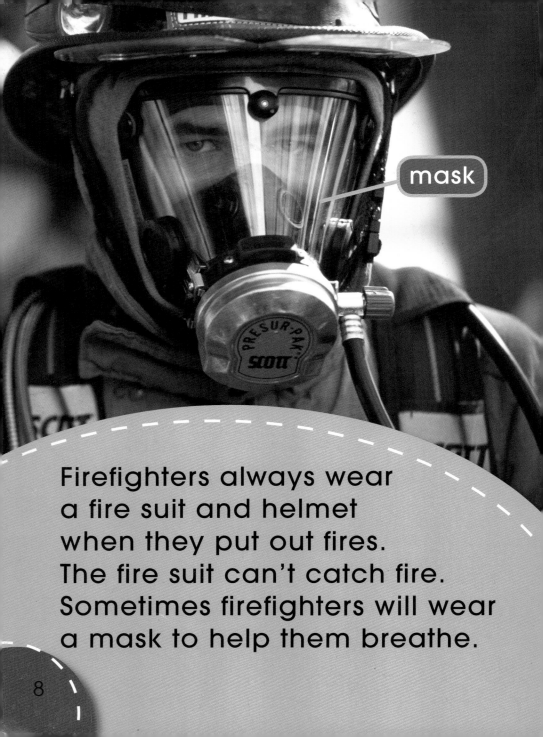

mask

Firefighters always wear
a fire suit and helmet
when they put out fires.
The fire suit can't catch fire.
Sometimes firefighters will wear
a mask to help them breathe.

helmet

fire suit

This race car driver
is wearing a body suit.
He is wearing a helmet
and gloves, too.

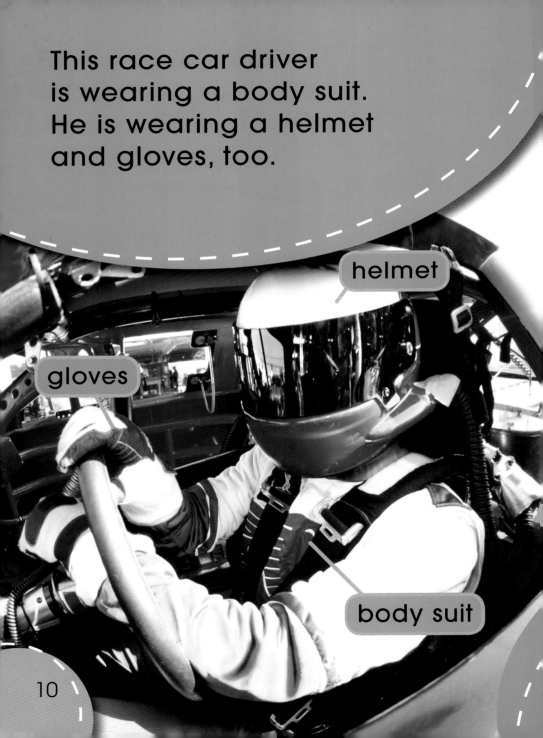

helmet

gloves

body suit

10

His clothes will help keep
him safe if the car crashes.

This suit is made
out of metal.
It is very strong,
but it is heavy, too.
A long time ago,
some people put on
suits like this
when they were fighting.
The suits helped to keep
them from getting hurt.

helmet

suit of armor

helmet

elbow pads

knee pads

Kids can wear clothes
that keep them safe, too.
Look at this kid.
What is he wearing
to help keep him safe?

Index

Guide Notes

Title: Clothes That Help
Stage: Early (4) – Green

Genre: Nonfiction
Approach: Guided Reading
Processes: Thinking Critically, Exploring Language, Processing Information
Written and Visual Focus: Photographs (static images), Labels, Index
Word Count: 211

THINKING CRITICALLY
(sample questions)

- Look at the front cover and the title. Ask the children what they know about clothes people wear to help them.
- Look at the title and read it to the children.
- Focus the children's attention on the index. Ask: "What are you going to find out about in this book?"
- If you want to find out about the clothes that help a firefighter, what page would you look on?
- If you want to find out about the clothes that help an astronaut, what page would you look on?
- Look at pages 8 and 9. Why do you think the fire suit can't catch fire?
- Look at pages 12 and 13. How do you think the suit kept the people safe while they were fighting?

EXPLORING LANGUAGE

Terminology
Title, cover, photographs, author, photographers

Vocabulary
Interest words: helmet, astronauts, space, divers, masks, gloves, driver, wetsuit, metal
High-frequency words: sometimes, always, time
Positional words: on, in, under, out
Compound words: firefighters, sometimes, wetsuit

Print Conventions
Capital letter for sentence beginnings, periods, commas, question mark